THE BIG SNEEZE
Ruth Brown

THE BIG SNEEZE
Ruth Brown

Oliver & Boyd

A **STORYTIME GIANT** book for shared reading

Oliver & Boyd
Longman House
Burnt Mill
Harlow
Essex CM20 2JE

An Imprint of Longman Group Ltd

Fourth impression 1995

ISBN 005 004391 9

First published by Andersen Press Ltd 1985
Storytime Giant educational edition published by Oliver & Boyd 1989

Set in Plantin Bold 22 on 26 pt.
Printed in Hong Kong
SWT/04

The Publisher's policy is to use paper manufactured from
sustainable forests.

For my father, Hugh Antonsen

One hot afternoon, the farmer and his animals were dozing in the barn. The only sound was the buzz-buzz of a lazy fly.

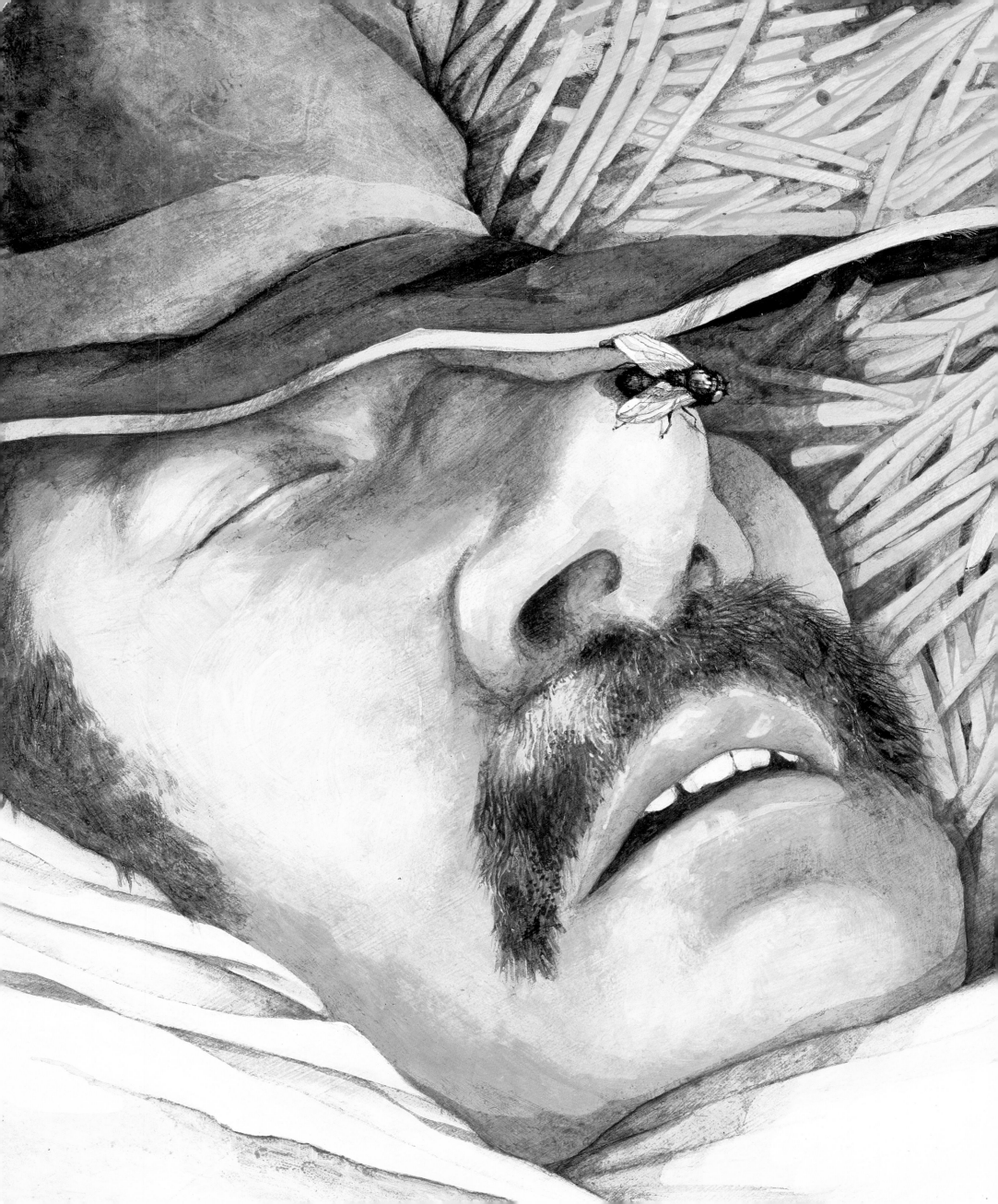

Suddenly the buzzing stopped —
the fly had landed right on the end of the farmer's nose!

"ATISHOOOOOOOOOO!" the farmer sneezed so hard
that the fly was blown high up into a spider's web.

This disturbed the spider,
who captured the fly —

which alerted the sparrow,
who chased the spider.

This wakened the cat,
who leapt at the bird —

which woke the dog,
and frightened the rats —

who fled from the barn,
chased by the dog —

which scattered the startled hens from their roost —

and panicked the terrified donkey!

"What on earth have you done?" shrieked the farmer's wife.

"Nothing, my dear," replied the farmer. "I only sneezed!"